P9-DDU-322

THE ELECTRIC SLIDE AND Kai

BY KELLY J. BAPTIST ILLUSTRATED BY DARNELL JOHNSON

Lee & Low Books Inc.
New York

LEE & LOW BOOKS INC., 95 Madison Avenue, New York, NY 10016
leeandlow.com

Edited by Kandace Coston
Book design by Abby Dening
Book production by The Kids at Our House
The text is set in Duper
The illustrations are rendered digitally
This story was inspired in part by the song "Electric Boogie" by Marcia Griffiths and The Electric dance choreographed by Ric Silver.
Manufactured in China by RR Donnelley
Printed on paper from responsible sources
10 9 8 7 6 5 4
First Edition

Library of Congress Cataloging-in-Publication Data
Names: Baptist, Kelly J., author. | Johnson, Darnell, illustrator. Title: The Electric Slide and Kai / by Kelly J. Baptist ; illustrated by Darnell Johnson. | Description: First edition. New York : Lee & Low Books Inc., [2021] | Audience: Ages 5-8. | Audience: Grades 2-3. Summary: Everyone in the Donovan family can dance—and has a dance nickname—except Kai, but his family helps him practice his moves to prepare for his aunt's wedding reception. | Identifiers: LCCN 2020013607 | ISBN 9781643790527 (hardcover) Subjects: CYAC: Dancing—Fiction. | Family life—Fiction. | Weddings—Fiction. | African Americans—Fiction. | Classification: LCC PZ7.1.B3674 Ele 2021 | DDC [E]—dc23
LC record available at https://lccn.loc.gov/2020013607

For Micaiah, my sweet "Cai," you inspired this book because you never gave up on trying to stroll with the AKAs! Middle to Middle — K.J.B.

To my firstborn son, Quin Ya'ir Johnson. Know that you were created by love and have a unique purpose that will impact the world. What you have to offer is needed and valued. Love you, son. — D.J.

“Well, it’s about time!” Mama says, waving a fancy paper in the air.

“What is it, Mama?” I ask.

“This,” Mama says, “is a wedding invitation!”

“Who’s getting married?” asks my big sister, Myla.

“Auntie Nina!” Mama says.

“To Mr. Troy?” asks my little sister, Ava.

“Yes, ma’am,” Mama says.

We all like Mr. Troy. He and Auntie Nina have been together forever.

Mama says that each of us will have a part in the wedding. Ava will be a flower girl, and Myla will be a junior bridesmaid. My older brother, D.J., and I will carry the rings.

"That's cool," D.J. says. "But all I know is that I'll be tearin' up the dance floor at the reception!"

"That's right, **D.J. Groove**!" Daddy says, calling D.J. by the nickname Granddad gave him. In the Donovan family, everyone has a dance nickname . . . except me.

I'm a terrible dancer! I can never get my moves right. At our family reunion last year, I tripped and knocked over my little cousin during the **electric slide**—that's our family's favorite dance.

Everyone was upset because they had to stop the music and make sure we were okay. After that I sat at a table while everyone else danced.

When dinner is finished, D.J. goes into the living room and turns on some music. Everybody forgets that it's his turn to wash the dishes, and they follow him. Mama and Daddy don't even look at their feet when they move right, left, backward, forward. Myla does a dip, smacks the floor, and *still* stays on beat with everyone else!

Daddy calls, "C'mon, Kai! Jump in this electric slide!"
But I shake my head. I'd probably mess up everything.

At bedtime I ask Mama, "Are you sure I belong in this family?"

"Of course you do!" She gives me a big kiss. "You are the special Kai part of our family."

"But I can't dance," I say.

"Baby, you are as much a part of the Donovan family as anyone. You've got your own rhythm, and there's nothing wrong with that."

Mama's words sound nice, and her hug is warm, but I don't want my own rhythm. I want the one everyone else has! How else will I get my dance nickname?

In the morning I wake up with a plan. I make a deal with Myla, who's the best dancer in our family—Granddad gave her the nickname **Miss Boogie**.

"I'll wash dishes for a week if you teach me how to dance," I say.

"This could be pretty hard," Myla says. "How 'bout two weeks?"

I sigh. "Okay, deal."

"First things first, you gotta feel the beat," Myla says, turning on some music.

"Right, right, left, left, then back."
I try to follow Myla's feet.

Right, right, left, left—wait, what?

I trip over my feet and fall down.

"Yikes!" says Myla. "Maybe we should take a break."

The rest of the week is exactly the same. Myla shows me the steps, and I practice them in my room after I wash millions of dishes.

"Yo, what are you doing?" D.J. asks one night, watching me from the doorway.

"I'm practicing," I tell him. "Myla showed me."

"Stop," D.J. says. "Myla showed you the steps, but you gotta come to D.J. Groove for that special sauce!"

"Special sauce?"

"Yeah," D.J. says. "You have to put your own groove on it, Kai. What's your special move?"

I shrug but then I wiggle my shoulders. D.J. nods.

"That's cool, but check this out!" he says, spinning and dropping to the floor. "Now you try *that*!"

I do try, but the spin makes me dizzy.

D.J. shakes his head. "Just keep practicing," he says, leaving my room.

I practice day after day.

Even Daddy helps me, stepping with me so I can get the turns right. My dancing is getting better, but I'm still not as good as everyone else in the family.

One month passes, then two. Soon we're packing up to go to the wedding. It's a long drive, so I make a deal with D.J. to watch dance videos on his phone.

When we finally get to Grandma and Granddad's house, I'm both excited and nervous. I really want Granddad to give me a dance nickname.

"Hey, **Baby Bounce**!"
Granddad says, pinching Ava's cheek.

"And how's **Miss Boogie**?"
he says, grinning at Myla.

Granddad shakes D.J.'s hand.
"Look how tall you are, **D.J. Groove**!"

When he gets to me, Granddad covers my head with his big hand. "There's my Kai!" he says.

"Hi, Granddad," I say. No nickname yet, but I'm gonna show him what I got on the dance floor!

On the day of the wedding, Auntie Nina looks beautiful in her wedding dress, and my new uncle Troy looks cool in his suit. D.J. and I have to wear bow ties, which are annoying, but everyone tells us how handsome we are.

After the ceremony, we take millions of pictures until it's finally time to head to the reception hall. I hear music playing before we even go inside, and my stomach starts flipping.

Granddad's the first to get on the dance floor, and lots of Dancing Donovans follow him. I'm stuck in my chair, watching the crowd.

And then it happens—*the song* comes on.

"It's time, *y'all!*" says the deejay on the mic. "Time for the **electric slide**! Everybody up!"

Now's my chance! But what if I mess up? What if I fall again?

I get up and sneak out of the reception hall. Maybe I'll hide outside until the song is over.

It's a good plan, until someone taps me on the shoulder. "What's up, nephew?"

I turn around and see my uncle Troy.

"Umm, nothing," I tell him. "I'm just hanging out."

"Hmm, that's funny. I hear you're a pretty good dancer," Uncle Troy says. He points back into the reception hall. "So, you should be in there."

I give Uncle Troy a look. He must not have seen me dance before.

"Maybe you can teach me your moves," Uncle Troy says with a grin.

"For real?" I ask.

"For real," he says. "I'm a little nervous. I hear your granddad gives out nicknames, and I wanna make sure I get a good one."

"Me too!" I tell him.

“Well, let’s go get it!” Uncle Troy says. He holds out his fist, and I bump it with mine.

We walk right into the middle of the dance floor and take spots in the line.

Right, right, left, left, two steps back, to the front . . . now what?

I freeze, thinking I'm about to mess up. But then I see everyone around me smiling, not caring if they miss a step or two.

So I spin like D.J., dip like Myla, and wiggle my shoulders just like me.

There's no tripping, no falling, no missing a beat!

We spend another day with our family, and Granddad doesn't say a word about my nickname until we're about to start the long drive home.

"All right, **Lil' Slide**," he says.

"Is that my dance nickname?" I ask.

"Sure is!" he says. "You put somethin' mean on that dance, Kai. Just like a Donovan!"

For the whole car ride I can't stop grinning. I don't need D.J.'s phone to watch dance videos anymore. In my mind I just replay the video of me, **Lil' Slide**, tearing it up on the dance floor!